Mabel Dancing

Written by

Amy Hest

Illustrated by

Christine Davenier

WALKER BOOKS
AND SUBSIDIARIES
LONDON · BOSTON · SYDNEY

On the night of the dancing party, Mabel

blew bubbles in the bath while Mama dressed up

and Papa laced his dancing shoes. Mama blew kisses

and Papa did too, singing a song for Mabel.

"Shall we dance ...

shall we dance ...

shall we dance?"

When the bubbles were gone, Mabel wrapped
herself in towels. Then she buttoned Mama's
dressing-gown and it draped to the floor.
She put her feet in Papa's velvet slippers
that were green and she put
her nose to the mirror.

"I can dance," Mabel said,
and Curly Dog barked.

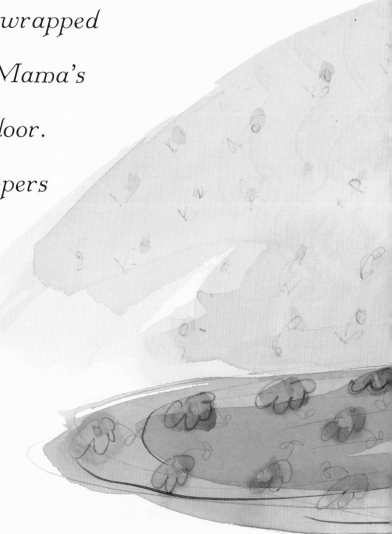

On the night of the dancing party,

Mabel was put to bed before the guests arrived,

and Mama tucked her in while Papa closed the

curtains. Then Papa tucked her in, and the

curtain blew and Mama's dress did, too.

"Sleep tight," they said.

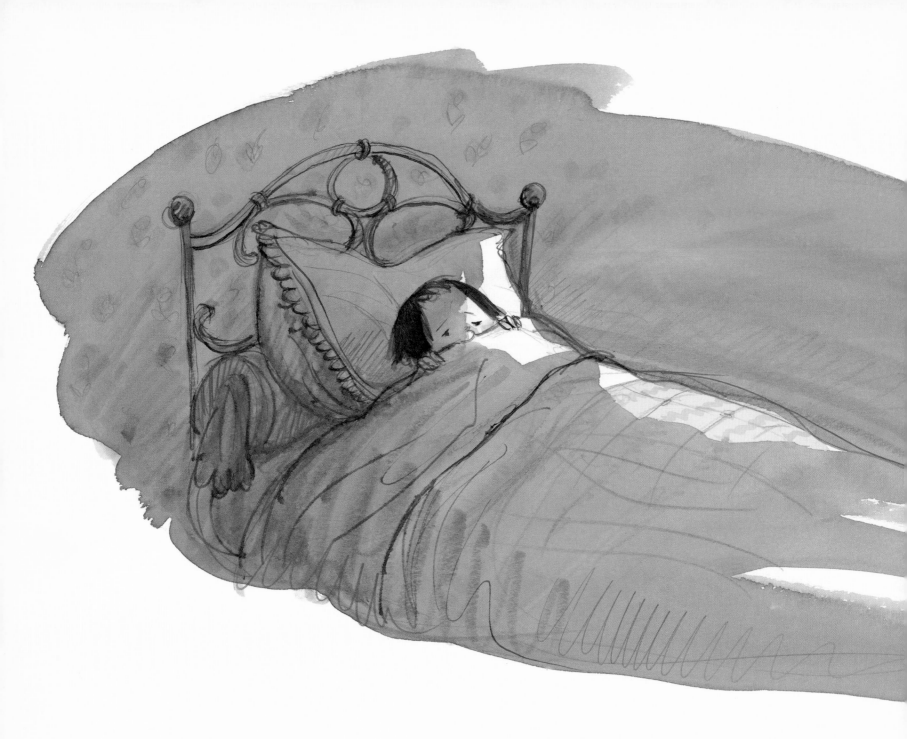

And there was Mabel, alone in the night.

From way down the stairs there was
music in the night and the music
had a way of floating up the stairs,

⁓ one, two, three ⁓

⁓ one, two, three ⁓

up and up the stairs.

Mabel hopped off the bed, hopping barefoot

to the window. Curly Dog came too, and

they stood by the glass, admiring the stars.

They counted Mabel's toes

and there were ten.

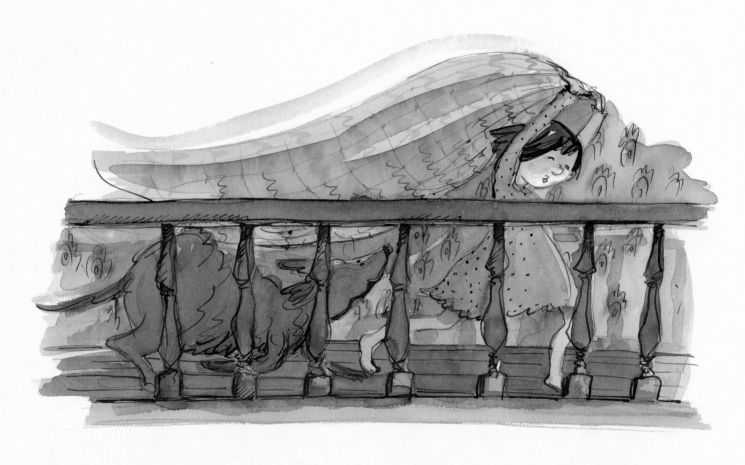

Mabel slid barefoot to the top of the stairs.

Curly Dog came too.

They sat down
and lay down
on Mabel's
yellow blanket.

From way down the stairs there was music

in the night, and papas in bow ties. Mamas

too, in swirling dresses, and the swirling

had a way of swooshing up the stairs,

⁓ swirl, two, three ⁓

⁓ swoosh, two, three ⁓

up and up the stairs.

"You dance," Mabel said.

Curly Dog yawned instead,

thumping his tail on the blanket.

Then Mabel stood up.

"Watch me!" she said, and off she went,

⌒ one, two, three ⌒

⌒ one, two, three ⌒

dancing down the stairs,

and she didn't make a sound,

⌒ shhh, two, three ⌒

⌒ shhh, two, three ⌒

down and down the stairs.

Mabel twirled and jumped in the bright
party light and her blanket blew up
like a yellow cape in the wind,
making swirls.

And Mabel had a way of

spinning past the guests,

— spin, two, three —

~ spin, two, three ~

floating through the rooms.

Mama and Papa loved the show, and so did the guests. Mabel bowed in her red nightdress.

"Shall we dance?" Papa said,
and they all danced away
in the velvet light.

Mama's dress swooshed and Papa's bow tie

tickled and they danced up the stairs,

— one, two, three —

— one, two, three —

up and up the stairs, with Mabel blowing kisses.

On the night of the dancing party, Mabel

snuggled way down deep in the big blue bed.

Curly Dog snuggled too. Mabel closed her eyes,

and the curtain blew like a yellow cape in the wind,

making soft yellow swirls.

And from way down the stairs ...

the music played on,

❮ one, two, three ❯

❮ one, two, three ❯

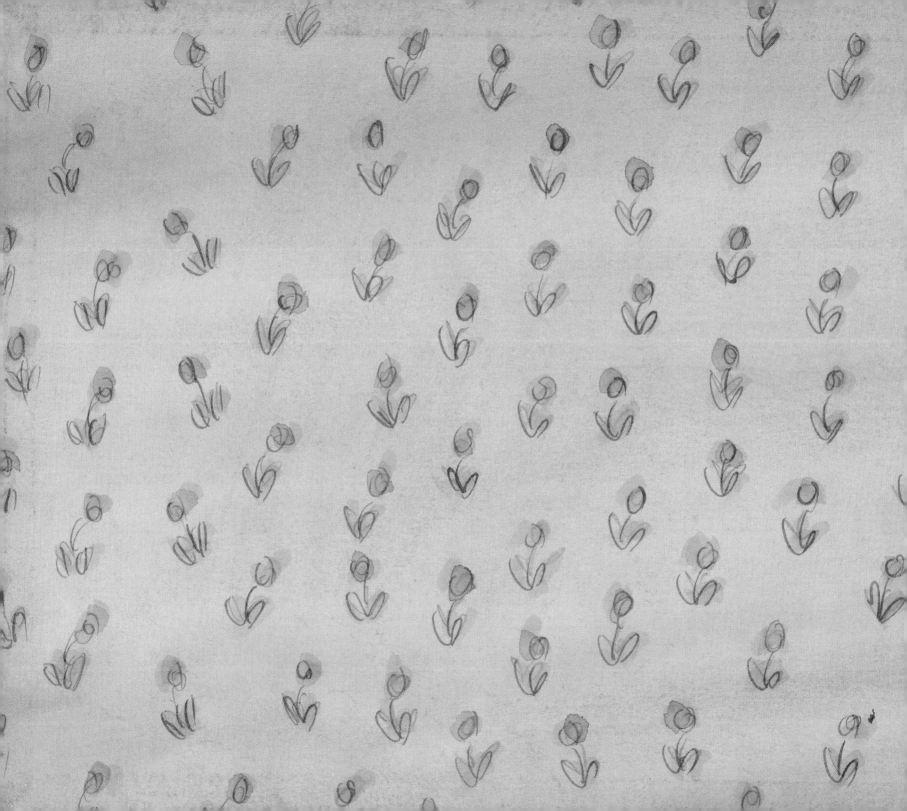